Twice Shy
The Restraint Series, Voume 1

By Jill C Flanagan

(formerly published under the penname Jill Christie)

Wyrd Publishing, 2nd Edition, 2014

Thank you to my Mom for always being a sounding board, and to my Dad for being himself; I love you both very much.

To my fellow writing buddies, I wouldn't have gotten this far without you.

Visit my website where you can follow me on my writing and weight loss journey at http://www.jillcflanagan.com or follow me on Twitter (@JillCFlanagan).

About the Author

Jill has always loved writing and reading. And she has always been curious about sex.

When she was young, she would try to discover things about sex by trying to find the naughty bits in the books she was reading.

Exasperated that Nancy Drew didn't do anything with Ned Nickerson, she moved onto more adult fare. And was confused as all the sex scenes were behind closed doors. Or worse, the prose was filled with euphemisms that didn't make any sense (especially when you didn't have intimate knowledge of the equipment involved).

Besides Jilly Cooper, she was pretty unsuccessful at finding out (from books) how sex really worked.

Many, many years later she discovered the joys of erotic fiction. She had all ready figured out how sex worked by then, but enjoyed the variety of situations and positions, not to mention the numerous perspectives.

Then she started writing it. Her world has never been the same since.

Chapter One

The weathered 'Bandit Creek Welcomes You' sign appeared by the side of the road. Stacy wished she had a shotgun to blow it away.

Westcott noticed her tension even though his eyes were searching for the exit from the highway. "It's all good, lovey."

Stacy slanted a frown at West and raised an eyebrow. He chuckled, knowing she hated the phrase. Annoying her would lessen her unease.

Stacy gritted her teeth at well-worn clichés and lies. She liked the truth, even if painful. She preferred being open and honest, but hardly ever blunt.

At first glance, she looked trapped in the 70's: a hippy chick/new-age wannabe. Upon closer inspection, the tailoring became apparent. Gauzy or gently flowing dresses and skirts and shirts, always nipped in at the waist and molding perfectly around her bust. She was a curvy 50's pin-up in a tailored 70's wardrobe. West was a young man during the era, and the clothes were ugly then and tacky now. Not on Stacy. Somehow it worked on her.

"I'm reverting back to my sixteen-year-old self. Pretty scary, West."

"We talked about this..."

She cut him off. "My head is aware I'm not being logical. You know the backwashy taste in your mouth? Not quite nausea, but close?" West nodded. Stacy continued, "I know I should be over it. I know I feel this way because it's the way I reacted the last time I was in this hellhole. Putting the knowledge into practice is another thing, though."

West looked over at his Stacy and wished he could have done this trip for her. "Well, fake it 'til you make it."

Stacy punched him in the arm, and her lips curved upwards slightly. She knew he was pissing her off on purpose. Poking at the obvious buttons. West was putting her in cliché purgatory as a diversionary tactic. She forced a smile again. "Love you, you old bastard."

West clasped her hand and squeezed with a brief pulse before he downshifted and took the first exit into her past.

Welcome back.

They turned into the Super 8 and Stacy silently let out her breath. They weren't staying at The Golden Nugget, where everyone gossiped about your meal choice at dinner, who you ate with, and how many times you went to the bathroom.

They had only decided a week ago the trip had to be done. She'd never wanted or expected to return.

She had become a runaway at sixteen. She had been lucky; she had somewhere to go. The new beginning turned out to be the best thing for Stace. She had found somewhere she could be herself. Not be labelled a freak.

She hadn't paid attention when West checked in. As they were walking into the hotel room she asked, "Are we in two rooms or one?"

"Adjoining, sweet." West made a Vanna White-like move to illustrate the door. Much campier than his normal behavior. He was doing everything to lighten the situation. Stacy's heart melted at the thought. He put his valise on the bed and stated, "If we manage to get what we want in a day or two, Tim won't join us. If we take longer, then..."

Stacy nodded. Tim and West couldn't bear to be apart for long. Tim, especially, suffered in West's absence. "How about I go next door while you give him a call? A full five bars on my phone means the coverage isn't bad here."

West shook his head. "I've texted him. I'll ring him later, he's busy with the club tonight since we're away."

That meant West was saving the conversation so the talk would turn into a long, lusty and private call. One with orders and maybe a little cock-and-ball torture in store for Tim. Stacy smiled, and added a bit of self-pity to the ton of emotions already roiling inside of her. Wistful and hoping she would one day be rewarded with the type of relationship Tim and West had. They'd been together for over ten years. A Master and submissive, who co-owned the club where Stacy worked managing the bar staff.

They were the gag-and-vomit type of happy 99% of the time. At other times they were committed and working out whatever they needed to. Stacy had benefited from their domestic bliss and was pleased for them. Except when she was navel-gazing and self-pitying, anyway.

"After, we'll demolish a bottle of wine and wait for Sarge. Then we can get a plan of attack."

Stacy nodded, breathing in deeply. She centered herself, took her time and became calmer, trying to let go of the anxiety. She emulated her Domme mindset by putting a steel rod into her spine and bringing her shoulders back. Reasserting her identity. Stacy was Miss S. Not forgetting who she used to be, but welcoming who she became.

West crinkled his warm hazel eyes, gazing knowingly at her. His look conveyed his belief in her. Confidence and confrontation were her strengths now. She hoped the surprise attack they planned to launch on "the bitch" would give them what they needed for Stacy to move on.

Sarge was a key component of the plan.

With her balance intact, Stacy nodded and gave West the first genuine smile since they'd decided on the trip to Bandit Creek. "I can't wait 'til Sarge gets here. It's been months. I wish he'd just move down to California with us and forget about the Cutters. I'm sure he would get a good price. He needs to sell and retire. Or something."

West didn't comment. Didn't have to. Sarge would do what he wanted when he wanted to, no sooner. All three of them at had at one time tried to convince their favorite ex-army blowhard to move down. Sarge became intractable when questioned, and refused to tell them why he preferred to stay in Bandit Creek. It continued to be a mystery, but to be tackled another day. There would be enough to deal with soon without worrying over Sarge's secrets.

Once they both settled, Stacy re-entered West's room through the adjoining door and cracked open the bottle of wine. They talked about nothing important avoiding the subject until Sarge came. They thankfully didn't need to wait long.

Stacy watched Sarge as he moseyed in, taking his time, taking the place in with his eyes, ever calculating. Sarge looked the same as always. His face had been stuck in middle-age ever since she'd known him, his skin weathered, deep smile lines bracketing his lips of his weathered skin. It had always amazed her how a man with thinning hair and pale blue eyes radiated such calm and self-assuredness. Sarge was appealingly grizzled, with his muscular frame, and was shorter than average. But he looked taller due to the way he carried himself.

West, aka Westcott Knowles, was six feet and wiry. With hazel eyes and silky coffee-colored hair that was worn slightly too long, giving him a rakish air. He was meticulously casual. Tim always complained to Stacy how long West took to get ready in the morning. He looked younger than his forty-seven years, his sprayed-on tan giving him a glowing visage.

Stacy thought about making a little small talk but decided to just get down to business and asked, "She still drinking most of her paycheck?"

"Nothin' much has changed, 'cept she's getting older. Still looks pretty hot considerin' how much she's abused her body. More cougar-like now. Goin' after the younger 'uns."

Not surprising. "She have a regular guy in her life right now? And do we have to worry about him?"

Stacy referred to Mary's talent for playing the damsel in distress. A certain type of man liked rescuing women. It was her mother's favorite flavor of man. Mary had a way of making the most ludicrous story plausible. Which meant if Mary went into the Saloon to pick up her pay, and she had a knight-in-a-shining-cowboy-hat in tow, the situation could easily become unmanageable. Mr. Cowboy Knight usually believed whatever Mary said.

Violence would ensue. The knight always fought for the maiden. Until he wised up, anyway.

The last thing Stacy, West or Sarge wanted was for the reunion to devolve into a physical fight. Their goal was Stacy's birth certificate. Mary's drama had to be managed.

Sarge answered, "She just broke up with a guy. He got sick of her shit. They sometimes still hook up. Billy shouldn't be there. And if he is, he won't be any trouble."

Problem was, Mary hated being cornered. If the male du jour wasn't around to defend her, rescuing her from persecution with fists or bluster, she would revert to her alternate weapons: manipulation, lies, guilt, evasion and even cruelty.

Stacy had the ability to handle those. She'd had sixteen years of practice. In the intervening time, her natural dominance and self-assurance had been nurtured. But the thought of confronting dear old Mom made her tired. The clock showed ten p.m., and she'd only had one glass of wine. Exhaustion filled her bones with an achiness which mimicked the sensation of 'flu.

Stacy stood and walked over to the two of them. "I'm exhausted. I'm going to go to bed." She kissed and hugged each of them and whispered "Love you" into West's ear and "Thank you" into Sarge's.

After Stacy left, Sarge made eye contact with West and shook his head. "This could be a clusterfuck, Westcott. Mary an' the truth don't reside in the same zip code."

West sighed. "I'm worried for Stacy's mental well-being. This is going to be difficult for her, but she needs a resolution to this. I hope Mary cooperates for Stacy's peace of mind."

"An' if you cain't get the answers Stacy needs?"

West remembered those first few months after Stacy had come to live with them. She hadn't even owned enough belongings to fill an overnight case.

After a time, Tim had started the process of ordering a copy of Stacy's birth certificate. They found no record of a Stacy Jones born in Montana on or near her birth date. Further investigation from a private detective revealed the same with a wider search. This weekend was about finding out the truth. No matter what. Either way West and Tim would take care of their own. Stacy was their family.

They had found ways around the situation. They had managed to get her into a high school with a bit of finagling. Work-wise, she worked under the table for them. But both he and Tim wanted their Stacy to have the freedom to do anything she chose to do. West and Tim both considered her their daughter.

"Tim and I discussed this extensively. We will try to obtain a ghosted identity if this doesn't work. We've got a lot of connections. Hopefully it's a matter of paying the right money to the wrong people."

Sarge stood. "We know she's gotta helluva lot of potential. She shoulda gone ta college. Papers like that're mebbe good for regular jobs. Wouldn't stand up to security screenin's though. No passport without frettin' about gettin' caught. I know Mary shouldn' have ever had a kid. She's not a terrible person, but she did some truly horrible things to Stacy. I hav ta get to work, make sure Mary shows up on time and Cotton don't intimidate the customers." He stretched and went to walk to the door. Stopped halfway and turned back.

West raised an eyebrow at him.

"There's 'nother potential problem. Brendan's in town. Surer than farts from a cow he'll find out our Stace is here."

West expelled an annoyed breath and said sadly, "This is going to be even harder for our girl. My poor, poor little girl. As if she doesn't have enough to deal with."

Chapter Two

Stacy lay in bed, beyond tired, but unable to find sleep. Throughout the years since she left Bandit Creek, she had excelled at compartmentalizing her life. Bandit Creek had become a small compartment, and she'd left it unexamined.

Being back here upset her equilibrium. She tried to focus on the soothing murmurs of West's posh English accent and Sarge's prairie rumble. After a while, the voices quieted.

Hearing a knock on her door, and West's smooth voice, she slipped on a robe and answered the adjoining door.

"Just checking on you, lovey."

Stacy sighed and leaned into West, trying to absorb his calm. She thanked the goddess every day Sarge had sent her to West and Tim. Her family. And even though she no longer lived with them, wherever they lived was home. They were the only two people in the world she allowed herself to show weakness in front of.

Especially Tim. He was a nurturer. "I miss Tim."

West kissed her forehead. He and Tim both knew she found it the most comforting thing in the world. Soft kisses to her forehead made her feel treasured and safe. "Me too, lovey."

She cuddled into him. One thing she loved about BDSM parents was they were free with physical affection. Kisses, hugs and cuddling were all for the taking.

"Get a good sleep. Shut off that brain of yours. It's all good." Stacy gave a 'bad-joke' groan at West's latest cliché.

She bundled back into bed, feeling cold. Montana wasn't cold, but it was freezing compared to California. Stacy was so glad it was June, and not winter.

Stacy felt more relaxed now that she'd had some cuddle time. She'd never had that sort of affection from her mother. Her mother got affection from the multitude of men passing through her bedsheets. Mary didn't really even acknowledge her existence most of the time. Stacy was dragged up, not brought up.

The only affection she had ever had was from her best friend, her only friend when she lived in Bandit Creek. Brendan.

And she didn't want to think about him. Coming back to Bandit Creek was hard enough. She could cope with everything else. Stacy was thankful she wouldn't run into him. Although she wasn't on it, she did a Google search which linked to his Facebook, so she creeped his profile. She saw he followed in his father's footsteps, just like his mother wanted him to.

A Forestry Warden, in Yellowstone. Hundreds of miles away from Bandit Creek. At least a six-hour drive. Thank the Goddess for small mercies.

Confronting Mary was going to be hard. Mom could compete on a national level when it came to guilt trips. Stacy knew she would view this as persecution.

Even though it had been eight years since she left, it sounded like her mother was still in the same holding pattern. Party, fall into bed and sometimes into love, alienate the loser she wasted all her emotion on and watch him walk away. Or wake up to an empty bed, sometimes with an apologetic note. Repeat.

Stacy had left. Fled was more the case. Thinking back to the day she left was still too painful. West and Tim had made her go to counseling to deal with all that. Bandit Creek was all about bad memories.

There were some good memories, too. Unfortunately, almost all of her good memories were tied to Brendan.

Isn't it strange how every good memory with someone could be tainted by one terrible act?

The counselor had advised her to focus on all the good memories. And she had. But thinking about the good made what had happened so much worse.

Because he had the same memories. And it meant their shared history didn't matter to him. That she didn't matter to him.

Logically, she knew teenagers made massive errors in judgment. But her heart couldn't be logical.

And what Domme could be logical about their first submissive? No matter how vanilla the BDSM play was between them, Brendan had been Stace's first sub. Yet the cornerstone of BDSM relationships was trust. When it was gone, salvaging it wasn't worth the effort. Usually.

She recalled a conversation she had had with West months after her arrival at his and Tim's doorstep. When she wasn't as feral. When she started to accept she was welcome. She'd finally learned what it was like to have a home. Her first.

She was having a little pity party, seated between the couple, but snuggled into Tim. He was a submissive, and in his past had endured abuse which was almost as depraved as a snuff film. Tim was hearth and home, with a face that would look more at home in a police line-up and a body that would rival The Hulk. He was a protective teddy bear when it came down to it.

West could explain things in a way that helped her understand better. "Lovey, no one ever forgets their best friend, their first love or their first sub. And losing each is a blow. Unfortunately, you lost all three at the same time."

There was a lot more discussion into the night, and a lot more cuddling.

She was half tempted to go next door and fall asleep in West's arms. He was a Master, as she was a Domme. But he was the type of Master all others looked up to. The über-Dom. Cuddling with him wouldn't be a submissive act. It would be receiving comfort from a father figure. Non-sexual, and truly safe and comforting. Even at twenty-four years old, she needed it.

In counseling, she learned she was starved for affection. There was a thing called 'touch-hunger'. Most people who grew up without touch found it difficult to receive. But in Stacy's case, it was the opposite. She craved touch. Since Mary hadn't ever given her any, she gorged on affection now. She always made sure subs she had scenes with received plenty of affection and aftercare.

Stacy had often wondered why Mary hadn't had an abortion whilst pregnant with her. Mary wasn't very religious, and she wasn't pro-life. The only thing Mary had strong opinions about was how to get her next drink and her next fuck. Preferably from the same guy. Stacy suspected Mary probably found out about her pregnancy too late to do anything about it.

Despite that, Mary must have cared enough to lay off the booze a bit, because Stacy was no dummy. She had taken online tests to see if she had any symptoms of Fetal Alcohol Syndrome, but she didn't. And her IQ was above average.

Stacy knew it was futile to hope Mary would be happy to see her. Until she was thirteen, she was locked in her room whenever Mary had company. Once her mother noticed she'd developed bumps on her chest, Stace became competition and her mother kicked her out until the next morning. Which probably saved her sexually, but not physically. If it wasn't for Sarge, Stacy would have probably died of exposure.

Stacy was not welcome at her best friend's house. Stacy was camp trash, and Brendan was from a middle-class home. So no matter what, she would never be good enough for Brendan. Danica Thomas was a schoolteacher, and a single mother, albeit in a respectable way. Brendan's Dad was MIA like Stacy's, but Mr. Thomas had a better excuse, since he was dead.

Camp trash was the Bandit Creek equivalent of trailer trash.

It wasn't as if Brendan had it easy. Mrs. Thomas wanted Brendan to be a Forestry worker, an idealized version of his father, Brent. Over time, Brent had become infallible and perfect. Except for the fact that he died.

So she couldn't run to the Thomases' house the first time she was kicked out when Mary was 'entertaining'. She ran to the only other constant in her life. Sarge.

Sarge was her mother's employer at the Cutters. But he was also a confidant. Like attracted like, and the Dominant in Sarge saw Stacy as she was: a confused girl who was scared by the perverted thoughts which ran through her brain. Not that she was old enough to even understand the craving to control, punish and dominate. Sarge recognized it and never said anything. She just felt safe to be herself with Sarge. They had a kinship.

Exposing their friendship was something which would have put Sarge in jail, though. Or at least at the center of some very malicious gossip. People wouldn't understand a middle-aged man befriending a thirteen-year-old girl.

So Sarge hired her to clean the Saloon up mornings. Gave her keys to the back entrance and to his apartment. And he let her use the spare room at his place over the Saloon. This gave her an excuse to be there early in the mornings, so it wouldn't look like she had stayed overnight.

Mary never knew where she went. Mary probably assumed she went to Brendan's house.

Sarge gave her a place to be safe and warm. Then, when it mattered most, Sarge got her out of town and somewhere safe. He sent her to West and Tim.

When she arrived on their doorstep, she was so happy she had a place to live she didn't even notice at first that West and Tim were a couple. A male-male couple was not something she'd seen in Bandit Creek. When the other shoe dropped, Stacy tried to act nonchalant and worldly, until she realized they didn't expect her to be. They pushed her to ask questions, no matter how hick her inquiries were. And there were some pretty rednecked queries.

The BDSM part of the relationship didn't become apparent to her for quite some time. All she knew about West and Tim was they owned a club. It wasn't as if they had a Master/slave relationship. Tim was only a submissive in the bedroom.

She tossed onto one side and then the other, plumping the pillow. Being back in Bandit Creek made her feel echoes of all the feelings she had when she was last here. Insecurity. Fear. Only now she didn't feel the need to fit in. Stacy knew she didn't belong here.

At times life here wasn't terrible, but that last day was so hard to get out of her head. Probably because the day before it was the best day she'd ever had up to that point in her life.

And being in the town where it happened was wearing on her. The sooner she and West confronted Mary and got the fuck out of Dodge the better.

Stacy needed to quiet her mind if she and sleep were going to even be passing acquaintances tonight. She sat up and went into a lotus-style position, leaning against the wooden headboard, feeling the ridge of it against her head. She controlled her breathing and tried to do a simple meditation. Anything to calm the thoughts.

Meditation was another thing that was suggested when she went to counseling, which was a couple of months after her exodus from Bandit Creek.

She remembered her panic when Tim sat her down to discuss it. She thought it was because she was too hard to live with. They wanted her to move on and were trying to fix her quickly so they wouldn't feel guilty about easing her out the door. After lots of prodding, Tim got that bit of paranoia out of her. Her leaving wasn't going to happen, unless it was temporary and with friends and a fully charged cell phone.

Stacy tried to be the perfect teenager so they wouldn't throw her out. It took some family counseling sessions with West and Tim to feel secure.

By the time she was seventeen, she wasn't as perfect. But she had been walking on eggshells practically from birth, and it was hard to do anything else.

Stacy felt herself go deeper into meditation, and started feeling calm and centered. Letting go of all her anxieties, she drifted in her mind, feeling restful and knowing she would be able to achieve sleep even though she didn't do a full meditation session.

She bum-walked into the middle of the bed, threw the covers over her head, and let herself drift. As she hung between sleep and consciousness, the memory came. The one Stacy couldn't escape. Especially now.

Soft kisses and soft touches on Brendan's bed. Blurry images and we're naked. He says, "Oh God Cee, I love your soft curves and body. Don't you dare lose any weight."

I smile and feel sexy; I believe him. He thinks it's crazy that others call me fat. He's wrong, but I love that he believes that.

Bren looks at me questioningly, and I nod. I lie on top of him. It's my first time. His too. I grasp his wrists and raise them over his head, urging him to hold onto the spindles of the headboard. He stays put. Our eyes meet as I grasp him and line him up with my opening.

He's my birthday present. My love.

I slowly sink on him, expecting pain, but none comes but the gentle stretching as I allow gravity to push me down. His hips start to surge upward. A widening of my eyes and he controls himself, stops, but it takes him a lot of effort. His face is a strange mix of pleasure and a grimace.

He knows I'm in control. I don't know why I have fantasies of doing it this way. But B doesn't judge. A part of me knows he craves being controlled. We're the perfect match.

I rest there, feeling his hips involuntarily twitch. We've been fooling around for ages, building up to, anticipating this moment.

It's been grasping underneath clothes, rubbing over jean seams, fogging up his mother's car windows.

Brendan followed my request. He masturbated a couple of times today so he wouldn't come too quickly.

I pull his hands off the spindles, his back arching as my shifting causes me to contract. It's getting hotter inside me. I can't tell whether it's him heating me or the other way around.

I use his hands to pull him into a seated position. "Remember, if you're close, tell me."

He nods. I lift my right breast and motion him to suck. He's done it through clothes before, and last time I almost orgasmed from it alone.

He sucks my nipple in, lets go. Lifts his left hand to my right nipple questioningly. I nod. He fondles my left nipple while he suctions my right.

Again I contract on him. And then again. And a long one after that. He stops. "Cee, I'm close, so close, I can't, I don't know..."

I push him down and lift myself off of him. I lie beside him, holding his hand until he tells me he's got it under control. A new condom is put on.

I'm still so wet, so he slips easily inside me this time. We do the same thing again. Sucking the left nipple and pulling gently on the right. My nipples must be attached to my clit because every pull brings that weighty, tingly feeling tighter low in my belly.

My breathing increases, which I discover makes me bear down on him. He stops, looks at me, pleading, desperate. "I don't think I can hold it this time."

I nod. His hips jerk up and down frantically. He groans, "Uh, fuck, Cee, oh god, Cee!"

I feel him spasm inside me.

After he recovers, I move his hand down to my clit. He moves in between my legs and spreads my lips open, fascinated by the way I look down there.

He follows my instructions–"Softer... oh, harder... try circles..."–the feeling in my belly is coiling tighter and tighter, trying to reach that painful barrier. My pussy contracts and I feel the muscles starting to undulate, tightening in ripples. "Oh B, put a finger in–oh yes, both at the same time. I'm so close, so close!" I am so near to that invisible barrier I have to pass to get to the orgasm. It's just out of reach. Unbidden, he puts another finger in and presses down hard on my nubbin. It hits, just at the right moment. I scream as I finally reach the pinnacle and I clamp down hard, my hips locking. I feel my release enter my bloodstream, my belly uncoiling, pushing warmth into my muscles and bones.

Bren plops down beside me and spoons me. Both of us are sated. We have a couple of hours before his mom gets home from school.

We skipped classes today for this. To have privacy together.

The rush I get from controlling him is almost better than the orgasm he gave me with his hand.

Fast-forward to the next day.

Brendan walks into the Saloon, where I'm cleaning, like I do every morning before school. I look up and smile at him. He smiles back, but there's a reticence to it.

He had football practice to go to after we made love, and I haven't seen him since we kissed and hugged goodbye.

I set down the mop and go over to hug him. His hug is the same as always. Warm, strong, safe.

He loosens his embrace, but is still close enough that warm air brushes my ear. "It's tonight."

"Why? Why do you feel the need to fit in with their stupid group?"

He lets go of me and turns away. "I thought I'd let you know so you don't think I'm avoiding you." He turns back and makes eye contact. There's a weird vibe with it, but I could be oversensitive because of what happened between us. "I love you, Cee."

I feel relieved. I reply, "Love you always, B."

It's not the first time we've said it. Does it mean more now?

Fast-forward again.

I'm in a car with Brendan's other best friend, Barton Ellis. The fact that he is an Ellis gives him a sense of entitlement as half the buildings in town are named after them. He is also a member of the Inner Circle, aka the IC. The group of guys Brendan's being initiated into tonight. Bart has never taken to me, nor me to him. We are allies only when it comes to Bren.

I say, "I thought the initiation was just for the IC."

"It goes down like this—there's five guys getting initiated, to replace the ones graduating next month. We park the cars around the initiation circle with the headlights on. He can't see you. But there's one witness who is..." Bart makes finger quotes. It looks strange on him as I wasn't sure before this moment he had the ability to punctuate. "'Close' to the Inner Circle pledge. They have to witness it. You were chosen."

I assume it's because Bart is in the IC. He would have probably been the choice if not.

Bart pulls up around the circle. Gives me a don't-fuck-with-me look. "Stacy, I swear, no matter what, don't make a fuckin' sound. He won't get in if he finds out you're here. And then where will he be?"

Better off, I think. But it's not what Brendan wants. He became a football player to become a member of the Inner Circle. He has always wanted to be a part of the IC. Another thing his dad was. Football player and all-around cool guy. Which is not how I see Bren. But I nod.

Bart gets out of the car. I see the guys, one of them Bren. I'm thankful it's warmer than usual for May, because they're naked except for...

And then I realize what Brendan's wearing. My underwear. The ones I was wearing last night. And he's got safety pins in them, so they don't fall off.

My face feels red. A sick wash comes up the back of my throat. I swallow to keep it and the feelings down.

I know now I've been set up. Bart has to be enjoying this. This is some fucked-up Carrie scene, but without the blood.

I should get out of the car. I shouldn't care Brendan won't get initiated. The foreboding feeling is getting stronger.

A voice sounds. I don't know whose it is. It doesn't matter. "Men, you are pledging tonight. You each entered the Dogfight and are wearing the dog's panties."

I don't know if I can keep from throwing up. I breathe through my nose and keep my mouth clamped. I just want to get out of the car and run. Go to the sanctuary of Sarge's place. I'm suddenly relieved I obeyed Sarge and didn't tell anyone, including Bren, I'm staying there. I kept it sacrosanct.

"You have the panties of who you've fucked and the committee has voted on who wins the Dogfight. The winner is... Tommo!"

Tommo. Brendan Thomas.

Chapter Three

The memories, once called, had become a mindworm. She'd managed to avoid replaying the worst part of that night. Stacy finally gave in to her insecurities and crawled in with West around three in the morning.

West waking her up at eight in the morning did not go over well. "Are you insane?"

"The complimentary breakfast food is not of high quality after 8:30 in the morning."

Stacy buried her face underneath the pillow and groaned. She loved West, but he was very particular about food. "You go. I'll have a protein bar."

West harumphed, and then continued in his best saccharine-flavored voice, "Lovey, breakfast is the most important meal of the day." Stacy sailed her pillow at him, which he dodged because her aim sucked. West smiled. "Now, see? You're awake now. Mission accomplished."

She sat up against the headboard and let her eyes adjust to being open. She patted the bed and West took her invitation and sat with her.

She said, "You're not used to small-town living. At breakfast, there's a possibility there will be staff from town, people I might know. Or who might know me. And then Mary will know I'm here. Word spreads in a small town like wildfire. Especially..."

West nodded and finished for her, "Especially since you're a part of town folklore, the way you disappeared."

Stacy breathed a sigh of relief. He understood and wasn't going to make her go have a proper breakfast. West was a big proponent of nutritious eating, a bit of a Californian stereotype. He was into whole foods and was a quasi-vegetarian. Which meant he and Tim ate fish and very occasionally other meats, but hardly ever beef. Eight years ago, coming from the place where beef was the only meat, that was another shock. She smiled, thinking of what a food fascist he was back then. Stacy had thought it was because of her weight. Having been made fun of most of her life, she was hypersensitive and had food issues. But along the way she came to understand West cared about health, not size.

As if he could read her mind he asked, "So what would you like?"

Eloquently, Stacy gave a "Huh?"

"If you think a protein bar will suffice for breakfast, you are mistaken. I will bring breakfast up to you."

Stacy decided not argue, but whispered "food fascist" under her breath.

Just before the door clicked shut, West said, "I heard that, lovey."

"Sorry!" Stacy yelled. Shit, now he's going to bring up yoghurt. Probably plain. Without fruit.

West was in a forgiving mood. He even brought bacon. He was probably feeling sorry for her because of the day ahead. Stacy was trying not to think about it.

Savoring the fatty goodness, Stacy thought about the task ahead. The Saloon opened at eleven-thirty, and Mary would be there first thing. If her mom hadn't changed her tune, Saturday was drunken stupor night. Her tips from last night would be long gone. It was Saturday, and there was partying to be done.

West, the prescient bastard, said, "You thinking about how you're going to approach your mom?"

"Trying not to. She's not all bad. I hope you know that, West."

West thinned his lips and gave her his 'Dad' look: "how many times do I have to tell you?" His 'Sir' look was more "obey or suffer the consequences". Similar, but coming from different contexts. Tim got the second, Stacy got the first.

West sighed, exasperated. "She was bad enough."

"But you're only getting one side of the story. She wasn't a great mom, but she didn't beat me."

Another harumph, and then West said in a gentler voice, "You can still be a terrible mother without beating. You know this, lovey. We've talked about it. I thought you'd moved the blame away from yourself."

Stacy felt herself tearing up. "It's this fucking place, West. I feel like I'm being haunted by the Stacy of Bandit Creek past."

West hugged her. "We can go home right now and not do this. We've talked about it. Tim and I can get you a ghosted ID. The best papers money can buy. Or I can go and confront her myself and you stay here."

Stacy shook her head, unable to speak or she'd cry. West brought her deeper into his arms, rubbing little circles on her back to pacify her.

"I hate you hurting, lovey. If I could take it away, I would. Let me take it away. We can leave. This was a bad idea."

It was so tempting to do that. Stacy had never thought she would have to come back here. She regained some of her composure and pulled away enough to look West in the eye. "No. I'm just having a bit of a weak moment. I need to do this. You know that." *And I couldn't do this without you. I wouldn't be strong if it weren't for you and Tim.*

West didn't look like he agreed, but there wasn't any argument from him. "Sarge said to be there at ten. Mary apparently gets there at about 10:30."

By the time they showered and both talked to Tim, Stacy was bolstered and ready to go. She was paranoid enough to convince

West to take the side exit out of the building.

The Saloon was only a couple of minutes away, like everything else in Bandit Creek. When she passed through the old swinging doors, the stale beer aroma flooded her nose. The place had been cleaned and the terry-cloth table covers had been removed and replaced with clean ones. Other than that, the place looked exactly the same.

Rough-hewn wood with knots and holes paneled the walls. Nicotine and varnish gave the walls a honey-warm patina. The floor was stained dark brown and had scuff marks from boots and moved furniture. Posters and stolen highway signs dotted the bar. The theme continued, signs displaying beer names long forgotten lying collage-like behind the bar itself.

The bar had hardly changed. Logically, it wasn't surprising, but emotionally it felt wrong somehow.

Tim echoed her thoughts. "Sarge, do you think you could bring this place into at least the late twentieth century? I haven't been in this place for over twenty years and I don't think anything has changed."

Sarge made a noncommittal noise from his usual place on a stool to the side of the bar. He sipped a coffee, probably his fifth or sixth of the day. Sarge wasn't much for sleeping and averaged at least one coffee per hour.

West grabbed her hand and gave it a squeeze. Stacy asked, "Where do you want us to wait so she doesn't see me?"

Sarge didn't seem very talkative this morning, which wasn't unusual. He pointed to the access door to the upstairs living quarters.

Stacy nodded, not feeling particularly chatty herself. Acid coated her stomach and she felt bile doing the backwash thing up her throat.

West put a calming hand on her back. "He'll text us when she gets here."

The next fifteen minutes did not go quickly. Confidence and self-assuredness were the cornerstone attributes of a good Domme. She was not in possession of those traits at the moment.

Once this was over, she could reclaim herself. It was this town. It was toxic. She wished she had taken West up on his offer this morning. Her only option was take West's tongue-in-cheek advice and 'fake it 'til you make it'. It felt false, but although Stacy believed in honesty, her belief in surviving was greater.

She needed to channel Miss S to pull this off with Mary. She looked inward and found her Domme. A moment or two passed and it didn't feel like she was faking Mistress S. Perhaps she wasn't.

Her cell phone vibrated in her pocket. Mary was here.

Chapter Four

After a minor altercation with West which she told him his presence during the confrontation would only complicate matters, they quietly sneaked down the stairs. She had lost the argument, but he had reluctantly agreed to stay in the background. Here was hoping he succeeded. Mary could muddy the issue like nobody's business.

West was protective of those he loved. When she locked eyes with him, she could see the crease in his brow ease once he noticed she had retrieved her head from her ass.

As she opened the access door, she heard Sarge's rumble, and Mary's flirty laughter. It was one talent she had always envied.

The voices drifted from the back in Sarge's office-cum-storage room with a desk. The voices were pleasant. Although Sarge never had liked the way Mary parented Stacy, he seemed to be able to separate that relationship from his everyday dealings with her mother.

Stacy was grateful to Sarge for so many things, it seemed wrong to begrudge him his usually cordial relationship with Mary. After all, it was hard to keep bar staff. And the elder Ms. Jones was a good worker if kept in line. Sarge had plenty of experience keeping people in line.

Stacy did sometimes begrudge him. The flip side was Sarge had kept Stacy's whereabouts a secret for eight years. Mary knew this, and to Stacy's knowledge, had not asked for her whereabouts.

She decided to make her ambush casual, as though showing up here was an everyday occurrence. West put his hand on her shoulder and squeezed as he sat down on one of the stools at the bar.

Moving behind the bar to the open office door, she looked in and saw Mary propped against a stack of crates, sipping a beer. Hopefully it was only the first of the day. Sarge sat behind the desk, leaning back casually, but his neck muscles were corded and his eyes watchful.

As she leaned against the doorframe, her curvy size-sixteen body blocked Mary's escape route. Out of the corner of her eye, she felt Sarge turn his gaze on her. Mary looked at her, smiled. "We're not open yet, hun." She half-stood, craning her neck. "Sorry, I thought I locked the main door behind me after I came in. Can I help you with something?" She'd used her flirty and charming voice. She hadn't recognized Stacy. It hurt. Using her cool head, Stacy knew Mary had written her off years ago, and didn't expect to see her daughter ever again. Plus, she'd changed a great deal in eight years. Honed the curves in her figure so she had a waist now. Tamed her unruly strawberry blonde hair. Found some fashion sense, albeit retro.

"Hi, Mom."

Mary's pleasant visage changed. She squinted, took Stacy in from top to bottom, and then focused in on her again. She stood, walked over and looked up into her face. Her voice hardened. "So the ungrateful brat comes home after five years. Sarge tole me you were all right and he's a man of his word. You couldn't of called? Written?" Mary turned around and flounced back to her beer and seat.

On the offensive. Mary wasn't stupid and knew there had to be a reason for this visit.

"Eight years."

"What did you say?" Mary asked.

"It's been eight years I've been gone, not five."

A moment of confusion passed over Mary's eyes and then cleared. "Same difference. So you obviously didn't come for money. Looks like you fell on your feet."

It was said in a sneering way. Calm, nodding, Stacy said, "I did."

The best way not to get pulled into a conversational eddy with Mary was to say as little as possible. Not to let her insults hurt. Not to let the hurt show if they hit the mark.

"Still fat though." Years of being called fat by Mary had taken the sting of that insult away. Her counselor had told Stace insults like that usually came from insecure people. She could never see Mary as insecure, but had accepted that she did this to make herself feel superior.

Smiling at this old trick in her bag, Stacy agreed, "Yep."

The smiling was a mistake. Grabbing her purse and standing, Mary said, "Well, it was a nice reunion, but y'all know I love my Saturday and Sunday off." She turned to Sarge and handed him her paycheck. "I endorsed this, could you give me the cash?"

Sarge leaned back in his chair and shook his head. "Sit down, Mare."

Mary blustered for a few minutes about him blackmailing her with the check. Sarge just sat there, saying nothing. She knew that he didn't have to cash it for her. She could wait like most people and put it in the bank and wait the three to five days for the cash to clear.

Moving back away from the desk, Mary asked, "May I at least go to the little girl's room?"

Sarge said, "Sure."

Mary walked over to the door Stacy was blocking. Sarge said, "No running away, Mary. There's some things that need to be said 'tween you an' Stacy. If you run away, Mare, don' come back."

Stacy's mom's back stiffened for a moment, and Stacy moved slightly away from the door jamb to make room for the still-petite figure to sashay through.

Whether she intended to bolt or not before Sarge's threat, the dyed-blonde bombshell came out of the bathroom a few minutes later and walked back into the office. She sat again. "I want to git this over with. Whatever needs to be said? I never claimed to be a domestic goddess, Stace. Your life coulda been a helluva lot worse."

How many times had she heard that one? Stacy looked at her, using a calm voice. "It's simple. I want my birth certificate. That's all."

Mary stilled. Her eyes looked left and then right, and then left again. Finally, her eyes rolled up and to the left. The sign of a lie in the making. Watching submissives had taught Stacy the signs of dishonesty: she had to make sure they were not over-exerting themselves, confirm they were being honest, not only focusing on pleasing their Domme.

"I lost it. You'll have to order a new one."

A lame lie. "We tried that, Mary. Turns out no one of my name was born on that date in this state."

Up and left again, then Mary put a reassuring look on her face. "Oh, hun, that's because you were born in Idaho."

"Looked there, too."

Before Mary could come up with another lie, Sarge cut in. "Cut the shit, Mare. Just try the truth for once."

Her mother looked like a scared rabbit. It was strange to see her frightened. Even if she ended up getting a shiny cowboy who liked to punch, Mary didn't ever act frightened.

She shook her head. "I can't. I can't tell you."

"Well, Mom, I need my birth certificate to work legally in this country. So you're going to have to. Please." Saying the please was difficult. But if saying got dear old Ma talking, Stacy would kiss her bum. She needed it. If she was going to travel or go to college, legal identification was a must. As much as Stace loved working for West and Tim, she needed to spread her wings before it was too late.

Mary looked over her shoulder. She'd been doing it a couple of times and Stacy wondered if she caught a glimpse of West or felt his presence somehow.

They were in a holding pattern, waiting for Mary to give up the goods. Sarge and Stacy were staying silent. Her mom was mumbling a protest every once in a while, but Stacy could tell she was going to spill the goods soon.

Mary looked over Stacy's shoulder once more. Posture slumping, Mary said, "Well, I guess I should start with the fact I'm not your mother and Stacy Jones ain't your real name."

Before the words fully registered in her brain, the door to the Saloon slammed open. Her body felt like it was thick and weighed down. She didn't even startle or look around. Seeing Mary's relief as she looked over her shoulder, Stacy wondered if she called for her off-again boyfriend as a reinforcement while she was in the bathroom.

Until she heard a voice say, "Cee!"

Mary had called for reinforcements, all right. There was only one person who'd ever called her Cee. Brendan.

Chapter Five

After Stacy was hit with that one-two punch, it took her a few moments to regain her equilibrium. Sarge stood, pulled Stacy in and closed the door as soon as he heard Brendan's muffled voice mixing with West's plummy one.

Dazed, she let Sarge put her into his chair. She heard him say some words to Mary, and they both left the office alone. She sat there for a length of time.

Her head wasn't processing quickly at the moment. She was still hearing Mary's words. She believed what Mary said though, because it made sense. Mary always felt put-upon for having to care for Stacy.

Sarge's and Mary's voices were added to the fold, ascending in volume, and then quieting into almost nothing after a few minutes.

And Brendan being here. As much as she kept hearing "Cee!" in her head like an underlying satanic track below Mary's words, he was not the priority at the moment. He was a problem to be dealt with, or not later. She could be mistaken anyway. For all she knew it was some drunk trying to get in before opening.

Telling herself she didn't have to deal with Brendan right now relieved some of her brain garbage. She surfaced. Having accepted what Mary said, Stacy noticed there were noises outside. Not arguments, just the everyday noises of the early drunks coming in for the day shift.

Standing, she walked on still-wobbly legs, each step getting surer as she moved to the door. Opening it, peeking out, she saw a bartender with a handlebar moustache whom she presumed was Cotton. Sarge was in his usual spot. Mary was in the first stool seat and West was in the second. Brendan wasn't in sight.

She wondered where he went. Or maybe she had imagined the door and his voice after Mary's revelation.

All three looked at her. She made a motion for them to come inside.

Mary placed herself on her beer crate. West wiped the unoccupied beer crates before he sat on them. Sarge rolled his eyes and chuffed a quasi-chuckle. Stacy sat on the desk, off center and near to the door.

"Talk." Stacy commanded.

Mary took a breath. "You ever heard of MM?"

Puzzled, Stacy said, "No, what is it?"

Sarge cleared his throat and Stacy shifted her hips so she could see him. "Montana Militia. Neo-Nazis."

Her non-mother nodded. "There's them in Montana, White Nations in Idaho. They're the big groups. There's smaller ones too. They're usually more fucked up. You were born in one of the smaller ones. Called Montana Freedom."

"You were born there too?"

Mary shook her head. "Family moved into MM when I was a kid. Then a few years later upped stakes and went to Montana Freedom. There was some fucked-up shit that went on there. MM was sane compared to Freedom. Ours was sorta a combination of survivalists and cult."

"Okay, so what was my name and date of birth so I can get a birth certificate?"

"You can't get a birth certificate."

"Why not, Mary?" Calling her that seemed strange on Stacy's lips.

"Because your birth wasn't ever recorded with the government. I was born afore we joined the camp. If I woulda been born in the camp, I wouldn't have a birth certificate either. You were born on the camp with a midwife. Patriots believe we are citizens of the state, and," Mary made air quotes and said the words in the same manner schoolchildren recite the Pledge of Allegiance, "Americans have been duped inta rejecting their sovereign status by unknowin'ly placing themselves unner U.S. jurisdiction through illegal contracts." Jurisdiction sounded more like 'jurisdicshun'.

"What in the hell does that mean?" Stacy was getting agitated.

Sarge cut in again. "To them, an 'illegal contract' is somethin' like a birth certificate, social security card, even a driver's license."

"So what was my name? And how in the hell did you end up with me?"

Mary shook her head. "Nuh-uh. Don't matter. You can get a fancy lawyer to help you." She looked at West. "Looks like your sugar daddy has some bucks." She eyed West up and down and turned her body to him. Sarge chuffed again. Stacy gave him the evil eye but he shrugged.

West looked straight into Mary's eyes. Whatever his eyes said it sent the appropriate message and her non-mom moved back into her former position.

Stacy decided not to clarify her relationship with West. But she persisted. "Why did you raise me?"

Mary looked defiantly at her. "You know when I said life coulda been worse? If I wouldn't have gotten you out and left myself, who knows how you woulda ended up? My sister was only thirteen when she had you. And she died because the fuckin' midwife didn't know what she was doin'. I was only seventeen when she died. Our mom was long gone, ran off with someone else when I was five. Then Daddy got with these Patriots. I decided that I needed to get out. And I couldn't not take you. Didn't want you, but couldn't leave you there. So I left with you when you were six months old. You had the croup, and I was allowed into town to get the medicine. So I hid and took off. Hitchhiked. Ended up here and stayed."

"Why didn't you give me up? Leave me at a hospital somewhere?"

Mary got a sour look on her face. "Wish I woulda thought about it when I first ran. Once I was in Bandit Creek, I was stuck with you. I liked it here."

It didn't sound like the whole story, but Stacy was exhausted. She looked at West, who noticed and then crossed the room to her. "That's enough for now." He looked at Sarge. They didn't say anything but some sort of communication passed. "Let's go, lovey."

Stacy was glad of the reprieve. They walked outside and to the rental car. They were silent on the drive to the motel and the walk (through the front entrance this time) to their rooms.

She slumped into one of the chairs in West's room. He nudged a drink into her hand. Looking down, she frowned. "Orange juice?"

"Screwdriver."

Shooting him a grateful look, she downed it and reached out for a refill. West complied, handing it back. "Sip this one."

Stacy felt the comforting burn of the vodka. "Was I hallucinating, or was that Brendan who barged in the door?"

"Mary texted him. Turns out he checks on Sarge and her every time he's in town to see if they've heard from you. Sarge doesn't tell him anything. This is the first time Mary has had something to tell. He could have been quite the diversion."

Stacy nodded, sitting there quietly. West got on the phone and ordered pizza. After he got off the phone, she said, "Wow, sympathy junk from the food fascist."

West nodded. "Pepperoni and mushroom. Didn't even order a vegetarian."

Stacy whistled. Any other time it would have been enough to shock her.

"Once you get some non-nourishing food into you, I want you to have a nap." He looked at Stacy's face as she was gearing up for an objection. "Stace, let me take care of you. You need sleep. I'm even going to give you half an Ambien. Then I can talk to Mary when she's three sheets and see if she'll give up anything then."

"What will I be doing while you use your manly wiles?"

"You need to at least talk to Brendan, even if to tell him to go to hell. Or say all those things in that letter your counselor made you write to him. Hell, kick him in the junk, or shag him to get him out of your system."

"I don't need to get laid."

West raised an eyebrow. "Oh? Remember who owns the club. You may scene privately with your submissive of choice, but it doesn't mean I don't hear more about your sex life than I want to hear. Apparently it hasn't occurred for quite some time." He shuddered.

Stacy colored and grumbled something of it being none of his business.

Mildly Westcott said, "It's not my business. Just like it's not my business what you do if you shag or scene with Brendan. I trust your judgement, lovey. By the way, why did he call you Cee?"

Stacy shrugged, slightly cringing at the name. "It's kind of corny. It started when we first became friends. We were from Bandit Creek. Initials being B.C. Brendan's name started with a B, mine ended with the sound of Cee. Two halves of a whole and all that. Together we were B.C. It's all kids' rationale, which really doesn't ever make sense. But it stuck. He was B and I was Cee." West gave Stace a somewhat empathetic look. Stacy asked, "How did you get rid of Brendan?"

"He's a very polite young man." Stacy rolled her eyes and decided not to comment. West qualified his previous statement. "He's a complete and utter tosser for what he did to you. Anyhow, he said he'd be in the bar from eight o'clock and he hopes to see you there."

***

Brendan paced back and forth. She was here. Cee was here. It was blind luck he was in town. His mom had guilted him into a visit during his rotation off. He had been planning on either heading up to Glacier National or venturing further north into Canada.

He'd rehearsed the apology thousands of times in his head over the years. Just getting to talk to her would be a start.

The guy who sent him on his way looked like a man of his word. He hoped that his message was passed on. He had waited down the street in a stalker-like manner and followed them to the Super 8. If Cee didn't show he knew where to find her. He wasn't letting her go without seeing her at least one more time.

A soft knock on the door. "Brendan?" Danica Thomas opened her son's bedroom door. "I just got off the phone. I heard that Stacy Jones was back in town. Is it true?"

He could see the concern on her face. See the words she was holding back: "I thought we had finally gotten her out of your life." Knowing those words would alienate him.

Brendan nodded. "Whatever you're biting your tongue about, Mom—just remember my personal life is exactly that—mine. I respectfully request you keep out of it. I make my own choices now. I hope I don't need to remind you about some of the paths you forced me down." Brendan pointed to his throat and gave her a meaningful look.

Her face clouded. She paused, looked defeated and nodded. She turned and left the room.

He looked at the clock. Still a few hours to go before they met up. Those hours would be interminable. He hoped Cee would at least hear him out. Let them try at the very least a friendship again.

He belonged to her, and she to him. Brendan just had to do his damnedest to convince her. He knew Cee didn't trust easily. He'd have to jump through every hoop to build trust back up.

Chapter Six

After the vodka and the carb binge, Stacy didn't need the Ambien. She hadn't slept much the previous night. West knew Stacy had an affinity for naps. She tended to burn the candle at both ends and supplement her sleep debt with afternoon pre-work snoozes.

Waking up later, Stacy noticed the connecting door was closed and she hoped West had napped also. She decided that having a long soak in the tub was in order before she had to "tart herself up" as West would say.

After rinsing out the tub just in case the chambermaid had missed it (there were some habits she picked up from West) she filled the tub and soaked for a while.

Baths were second only to afternoon naps in Stacy's opinion. She showered after going to the gym, but baths were for soaking the brain and the body. They were also a great way of getting rid of sexual tension. Although she didn't particularly like "There's Something About Mary", name notwithstanding, she agreed with the theory that a little masturbation went a long way. It stopped her pink parts from ruling her head.

The only problem with getting off was that she usually fantasized about a former sexual experience. And the most vivid movie playing in her head at the moment included Brendan.

He had sneaked into her head here and there during her do-it-yourself orgasms. She tried to push him out of there, but it rarely worked. The harder she fought it, the more her psyche battled to keep him there.

She could call any of the subs she knew and get sexual satisfaction. But Stacy didn't really like sex without some sort of emotional connection. Even phone sex.

She was popular at the club. Stacy wasn't into humiliation and didn't like inflicting anything but pleasurable pain. She loved cock-and-ball torture. Loved controlling a man's orgasm. Loved getting her submissive so close to orgasm and bringing him back. It was the best thing about being a Domme, giving that gift to the sub, engendering trust between them.

Instead of thinking of anyone in particular, she decided to try to think about no-one. Closing her eyes and soaking up the heat in the water, she inched down her body, stroking her tightening nipples, and glided her right hand down her rounded belly to her pussy lips. Bending her knees, she decided not to make it sensual. Just down and dirty. Letting her still-closed eyes look into the blackness behind her lids, breathing deeply and centering herself. Forcing all other thoughts out of her head, she then started rubbing her clit slowly while breathing deeply in and out, contracting the walls of her vagina at the same time.

She felt the lovely familiar feeling coiling in her lower belly and took her finger off the good spot for a while, knowing if she laid off at the right moment during the build-up the orgasm would come faster when she started again.

Feeling the not-quite-oily wetness between her legs, she again started out on her clitoris, rubbing in staccato-like circles, lightly interspersing a bit of tapping with rubbing. She concentrated on her breathing as it contracted her vagina in a way bearing down didn't. She felt the heat radiate over the front of the hipbones, lifting her hips and then taking her palm and pressing it hard down while using the other hand to press down firmly above her triangle, pointing her toes to bring on a better sensation.

Then she came suddenly. The spasms, the inner legs contracting along with her insides, muscles freezing altogether in a rictus while she came.

Resting her body in the now cooled water, Stacy waited until she recovered to stand. She then got on with the business part of her shower.

Unfortunately in those last moments, all the thoughts she forced out of her mind were for naught as her mind chose to show her the face that she really didn't want to see when she was coming. The man who betrayed her. The man she really didn't want to want. But did.

Getting out of the shower, she supposed it was inevitable in a karmic sort of way that Brendan would have to be here when she came back to Bandit Creek. He was the one person she still wanted to see. Also the one person she wanted to take every step to avoid.

He'd already stomped on her heart once.

After taking way too long to style her hair, find the perfect bra and panties, then top them with a dress and don't-fuck-with-me boots, Stacy knocked on the connecting door. West slightly opened it, his ear to his cellphone, and mouthed, "Ten minutes."

Which gave her much longer to fuss. Considering she wasn't really the type to obsess about outfits, hair and looks, she knew the cause was Brendan.

The thing with Mary was still whirling in her brain. She hadn't come anywhere near to processing it yet.

She wondered what it would be like growing up a Domme in a place where women were supposed to be subservient. It would have been so much worse.

Plus, she wouldn't have had West and Tim in her life without Mary. For that matter, without Brendan, she wouldn't have run away.

Not that she'd forgiven either Mary or Brendan. No way.

Yet she was looking forward to seeing Brendan too much. She didn't want to feel like that.

West knocked and opened the door slightly. "Ready, lovey?"

Stacy didn't say anything, she just walked up to West and held out her hand. He took it, kissed it and they walked out of her door.

On the ride over, West gave Stacy a snapshot of the work he had put into motion when she was napping, fluffing and peacocking. He'd told Tim the skinny and tasked him with chasing down a lawyer who could get her a whole mess of 'illegal contracts'. It would take some time and probably quite a bit of money, but it was already in the works.

"If that doesn't work, I have some higher-up connections."

Stacy raised an eyebrow. But some pretty famous and well-placed people frequented Restraint, West and Tim's club.

Stacy shook her head, thinking again what it would've been like to grow up a member of Montana Freedom. Being molded into an anti-government racist. She shivered at the thought. She would hate people like Tim and West because they were gay and were involved in an alternative lifestyle.

Stacy was relieved she wasn't going to have to live her life with fake papers. Knowing her personality, she would have looked guilty every time someone asked her for her faked driver's license or birth certificate. Now, she had a new future to consider. A flare of excitement burst in her belly.

Parking was full outside the Saloon. It was nine p.m. and the Saturday night crowd was already there.

And Mary and Brendan were inside. Except Sarge, Stacy didn't care about anyone else in this town so she didn't worry about it. They walked up to the bar to greet Sarge. Never failing to get to the point, Sarge said, "Mary's at two o'clock and Brendan's at five."

Stace turned around to look for Brendan and he was on his feet, cautious as he walked to her, trying not to spook her perhaps. She looked at him. He'd filled out, not tremendously, but what he had was honed. He had on what looked like a soft brown t-shirt and barely blue jeans, so broken in they had almost been leached of color.

His chest was well defined on his six-foot frame. Nice biceps, not steroidal big, but large enough to convey strength. His jeans hung low in the front, low enough that when he moved, she could see the barest glimpse of belly. His caramel hair was in need of a haircut, thick and slightly shaggy, but not long.

His green eyes were as bright and perceptive as ever. As alpha male as ever. Many people thought a man couldn't be dominant in life and submissive in the bedroom. That was the best kind. The kind who wanted to take care of their mate, protect them, and then submit in the bedroom, knowing full well they could overpower their Domme at any moment if they so chose. Having a strong man submit? The sexiest damn thing in the world.

She turned her head towards him, and he sped his pace. "Cee." His voice sounded raspy, hoarse. Even that was sexy.

"Please don't call me that. Stacy or Stace will do."

He nodded. Looked deeply into her eyes. "Stacy, can we talk?"

"What do you want to talk about?"

"Just talk. About anything." His green eyes focused on her blue ones. Sending bolts of unwanted heat to her nether -regions. Swallowing hard, he said, "Anything. But if you let me I want to apologize. And explain. Not justify, but explain." He made a placating gesture with his hands as if he thought he would spook her. That Stacy would either verbally attack him or walk out.

She hated that she was still attracted to him. But West was right. They needed to talk over some things.

West walked by at that moment, his fingers brushing hers. "The things I do for love," he said with resignation as he headed towards Mary.

Another cliché. But true. He was flirting with Mary for her, trying to get a name. Her real name.

She returned her gaze to Brendan, who was patiently waiting. "I don't want to talk in here. I don't want to go to your mother's." It felt wrong after all this time to show him Sarge's place. "That leaves my motel room. Come on, you can give me a lift up there."

After telling Sarge where she would be, they left. Brendan opened the door for her. He was coiled tension, clenching and unclenching his keys in his hand as if they were an exercise toy. Stacy could tell he didn't want to screw this up; he wanted forgiveness. Stacy wondered if she had it to give. Thinking back to her counseling sessions, she was always told letting go and forgiving were better for Stacy's own emotional state. Doing so wasn't always about the guilty party, but about her.

Maybe there really was some truth in that. She didn't feel the resentment she'd expected to experience for Mary or Brendan. She didn't like Mary much and hadn't totally forgiven her. Or him. Thankful for where her life ended up. Maybe coming back to this shit-hole was cleansing. Who knew?

By tacit agreement, nothing was said until they were in Stacy's room. Thankfully it wasn't a mess inside. Years of Tim and West's combined tidy genes had rubbed off on her. Some.

Stacy sat in one chair and motioned Brendan to sit in the other.

Silence ensued for quite a long time. Stacy was looking at Brendan, seeing again how he'd physically changed in the past eight years. The soft look teens' faces had was no longer there. The muscles he had were mostly veinless. Not bulging, but well defined in a soft layer of smooth skin. A brush of dark brown arm hair had sprouted at some point, lightly furring his arms but not his hands.

He was even better-looking now then back in high school, the bastard.

"So." Stacy prompted Brendan.

Brendan took a breath, making eye contact. "I've tried to think of a way to convey how sorry I am, C–I mean Stacy. How do you apologize for it? All I can say is I've regretted it every day of my life since. I will do anything..." He swallowed hard, looked at her with determination and hope, his hoarseness even more distinct. "Anything, Stace, to get you back in my life."

That voice went through her like short fingernails scratching an itch on her back. So warm and tingle-making at the same time. Deep, manly.

She mentally gave herself a slap and shook out of the influence of that voice, sighed. "Here's the rub, Brendan. I don't doubt at all you're sorry. I just don't know if you're sorry because you did it or because I saw it."

Brendan shook his head. "You were the only one who ever believed in me. I wrecked that. After you disappeared, I quit the football team and didn't associate with the IC. I even cut off ties with Bart. Beat the shit out of him, or tried to after I found out what he did. I fast-tracked in high school, took summer classes and graduated a year early so I could get out of this place. Away from Mom."

"You became a Forestry Warden, still."

Brendan nodded. "I was. Hated the job, the bullshit. You know why I did it. Mom wanted me to be Brent Thomas number two. Plus I got this lovely voice from a forest fire. Damage to my vocal cords." He said it factually, without self-pity.

She wanted to make him feel better. Tell him his voice was sexy as fuck. Revert to old patterns when she championed him and vice versa. She wasn't ready to accept his apology. "I just don't understand, Brendan. If I meant half as much to you as you did to me... How could you dirty what happened on my birthday in that way? You were the only one I trusted not to make fun of me behind my back. It made me question every moment we ever had together. Did you laugh about me with Bart?" He opened his mouth, but she said, "No. I'll have to hope that you didn't. Because it hurts too much to think that you did."

The worst part of that night came rushing back to Stacy. The part she had tried not to remember.

After Tommo was declared winner of the Dogfight, they had allowed the guys to get dressed. All the guys were to recite the details of their sexual conquests with the dogs. She had wondered if there were other girls looking on in horror. If that was part of the IC's game.

"And finally, Tommo, tell everyone your Dogfight story!"

Brendan takes a breath and he looks uncomfortable. It gives me some solace. "So me and Cee hang out every day. She's a friend and all. I know she's had a crush on me for years. So getting with her was easy." Brendan holds up my panties. The ones he had to use safety pins to keep on. Lots of chuckles and I see Bart looking to the car knowingly. "And she's into kinky stuff. She has fantasies about tying people down." The tears have made the front of my shirt wet. And still I'm trying to keep quiet, not wanting to ruin it for him. He's been my best friend since grade one. After all he is saying about me, I don't understand why I am frozen in place, unable to do to him what he is doing to me. I'll be the talk of high school tomorrow. The Inner Circle members will make sure of that.

I know now that Bart just wanted me to see this, that there weren't any other 'witnesses'. Other girls would be causing a scene. I'm the only one stupid enough to stay.

Brendan shrugs. "That's about it."

They all start crowding around the new pledges. This is my chance to get out. To leave. I quietly open Bart's car door, not closing it, and run away. Run to Sarge.

As the memory flashed through her brain, Stacy waited for Brendan's answer. It came eventually. "What I said to you was true. What I said to them was a lie. I wanted to be in the IC so badly I didn't look past the moment. I won't put it down to me trying to live up to my dad. I won't excuse it. I was a dumb little shit. I never thought of what the consequences would be for you. I realized it after you left town. Actually, Sarge made me realize. I also figured I could somehow find out a way to keep you and the IC in my life. I didn't know how. I hadn't thought that far ahead.

"Saying that, when we were together. Having our first time together..." Brendan cleared his throat and paused. "It confused me. And I did have some hard feelings about it. I used those feelings when I was telling the IC about us. It was the best thing that had ever happened but I felt—less manly. I didn't understand."

Stacy nodded, softly said, "Neither of us understood. We just went with our instincts. Enjoyment of being dominated can be confusing. I can see it. I didn't know I had to ground you after. It's called giving aftercare. Taking care of you and making sure you don't have yo-yo emotions."

Brendan asked, "Do you... um, dominate that West guy?"

She laughed. Brendan looked confused. "West is like a father to me. He and his boyfriend took me in when I ran away." Brendan looked relieved. "He's a Dominant. So am I. Have you ever been submissive to anyone else, or are you vanilla?"

He looked a bit embarrassed. "I went to a Munch, you know one of those potlucks for people wanting to know more about the life? I went to a couple of parties after and watched." Brendan shrugged. "I know I am a sexual submissive, but I haven't ever had sex that way. Well, except..." His voice trailed off. Then more quietly, "I was hoping someday I would see you again. And we could try again. That you would forgive me. I still love you, Cee."

Stacy didn't know what to say at first. Part of her wanted to erase the past and forgive Brendan. But it wasn't that easy, was it? No. "I can almost believe you mean that. But you love the sixteen-year-old. That girl is gone. I'm the bitch who lives in her body now." Stacy said it with a smile, so it wouldn't come across harshly.

Brendan shook his head. "I don't think there's anything you could do that would stop me loving you, Cee."

"Stacy," she gently but firmly reiterated.

All those years of shared friendship were harder to discount when he was sitting right across from her, his hands tucked between his legs so he wouldn't touch her. Such obvious body language.

He was still so gorgeous. More so, even. Stace wanted to touch him so badly. Wanted to see if his actions followed his words. Standing, she motioned him to stay put. Moving her chair in front of his, she seated herself. She put a finger against her lips and then stretched her hand out.

Brendan gave her his hand. Stacy delicately traced each finger, feeling the little hairs on his hand stand to attention. She turned it palm up, drawing light circles over the hard callouses.

She could hear his breathing increase. The simplest acts of domination could be the most effective. He squeezed his legs together to maintain control. She could see the outline of his cock getting more distinct against his jeans.

Bending her head over his hand, she pressed a soft kiss in the middle of his palm. His fingers involuntarily contracted as Stacy lifted her head. His pupils had dilated. It was obvious he wanted more. He'd used all his control not to move.

Having put his hand down, she moved her chair back and resettled herself.

Brendan's eyes were confused. "What was that?"

In her Miss S voice, Stacy asked, "What was that, what?"

His breathing increased, his chest movement was more rapid. In a choked voice, he said, "Mistress."

She corrected him. "I'm not your Mistress yet. Call me Miss or Miss S. It was a test to see how you respond to dominance. You might have changed over the years. At this moment, it's far as I'm willing to go with you. We're leaving tomorrow." She could see the objection starting in Brendan's face and made a hand motion to show him she wasn't finished talking. Stacy had decided how far her forgiveness would go. "I don't know if I can forgive you, Brendan. I want to. But the responsibility will be yours. I'll give you my phone number and email. I will never live in Montana again. California is home. Text me and give me your schedule every week, informing me of when you are available. You told me you quit the Forestry Service, what do you do now?"

Brendan told her briefly about his work in the oilfield.

"I will use the schedule and choose when and where to call you. And you'd better answer. I know you don't really take orders out of the bedroom. But I will push you. It doesn't mean you can't push back. But remember, you can discontinue the relationship at any time. As can I. It's your second chance, Brendan. There will not be a third. Think of the consequences before you text me your schedule. I don't hear from you by midnight tomorrow, it will mean you have decided not to pursue this."

Stacy stood, signaling him to leave.

"I'll text you tomorrow, email, and leave a voicemail. I don't want a communications mix-up." He looked at her, happiness in his eyes, his dick still bulging in his pants. "I want this." The sincerity was almost Hallmark movie-of-the-week in its conviction.

As she let him out the door, she said, "Oh, and Brendan?"

He looked up.

"No masturbating without my permission. Your orgasms are mine."

A look of disappointment and then grim satisfaction crossed his face. He nodded, and using that choked voice again, said, "Yes, Miss."

Good boy.

***

Brendan walked gingerly down the hall. Feeling exhilarated. Hopeful. Unfortunately every step he took rubbed against his hard-as-nails dick. Even so, he didn't care whether Cee dressed him up in drag and walked him down Main Street.

Well, he hoped she wouldn't do that.

It amazed him how she got him close to coming just by touching his hand. Once he was out of sight, he fist-pumped, happier than he'd been in ages.

In the near future, her creamy freckled skin was going to be his to touch. Those luscious generous breasts his to suckle. That perfect round ass his to knead. With permission of course.

He hadn't been celibate since Cee left, but he'd only had one relationship which lasted longer than a fling. Everyone he fucked tasted not quite right.

He was tempted during those house parties to try sexual submission out. But he wanted to save that type of sex for Cee. The thought of giving his control over to anyone else rang false, as did being in a relationship with anyone else.

He guessed he had that in common with his mom. She had never dated anyone else after his father died in a forest fire. She always said he was the one for her.

Cee was the one for him.

He pressed the down button for the elevator, forgoing the stairs, his raging hard-on making longer strides a bit too exciting.

A voice sounded behind him. "Tommo!"

Brendan cringed. Being in town meant that you inevitably ran into high-school comrades. Whether you wanted to or not. He looked down at his arousal. Fuck it, who cares what anyone thinks. He wished Cee were witnessing this. Hard-cocked and proud.

Turning around, he saw his once good friend. "Hi, Bart, what brings you to the Super 8?" Bren knew full well Bart had to be up to no good with a wife left at home.

Bart looked a bit worse for wear. The muscle built up in high school was more bloated now. Bart wasn't fat, but he no longer had the impressive build he had had back when he was lineman. The guy wasn't bald yet, although he had those receding scoops in his hairline.

"Hey, Tommo, you know the saying. What happens at the Super 8 stays at the Super 8, right? You wouldn't fail a man-test and go blabbing to Melissa, would you?"

Crossing an Ellis was not wise. No matter what problems he had with his mom, if he pissed off an Ellis, she would be the one suffering for it.

Bren shook his head. "Not my business, man." Turning back to the elevator, he hoped it would arrive soon.

Bart stood beside him. "You staying here or visiting?"

"Visiting. You remember Stacy Jones?"

"Shee-it, Tommo, I thought she was dead or something. I don't fault you for going for the soft landing, she's got to be a cushy ride. But she's just like her mother, camp trash through and through."

Brendan's fists were clenched tight. He could feel his nails breaking his skin on his palm. The pain cleared his head and made him think logically; it stopped him from belting the fucking asshole. He almost kneeled in thanks when the elevator finally arrived.

At least his penis wasn't as happy now that he'd seen and talked to Bart.

More soberly than his whiskey-laden breath should have allowed, Bart said, "By the way, anything she says about me is a lie. She's always had a hate-on for me, that one."

Bren asked, "Like what, Bart?"

"Nothin' important. Just mind my words." The elevator doors opened. "Nice seeing you Tommo, let's get together for a couple of sociables soon."

Brendan called out, "Hey Bart?"

Bart turned around with a sloppy smile, which froze when he saw the look on Brendan's face. "We may've been friends in school, but don't go thinking that we're still buddies. Stacy is a better person than you and me combined. Know this – I would kick the fuck out of you right now, or I would give it a helluva go. But if I did that, you'd get revenge by making life hell for my mom, because that's what Ellises do."

Bart was silent for a moment, then smiled, "I'll give you a free pass on that one, 'cause you're cunt-struck. I can see she's already been telling tales about me. You'll soon realize that she's lyin', and I'll accept your apology then. You have a good day Tommo."

Brendan would have to get to the bottom of this. Stacy might not know it yet, but protecting her, keeping her happy and safe in the world was going to become his responsibility again. Just like in school. Except this time he was going to do it well.

***

Stacy heard a bang next door. Easing open the adjoining door, she spied West sprawled half on the bed and half off, cell phone in hand, trying to use his voice command. He slurred his words, which sounded a little like, "Callshub." The voice command responded, "Did you mean 'Castle'?" West gave an aggravated "Nuh!"

Puzzled, Stacy walked over and smelled him and took his cell and disconnected it. "Oooh boy, West, you reek. How did Mary get you so drunk?"

West mumbled something which sounded like, "Yuggerbum."

She snorted. Thankfully being a bar manager gave her a degree in drunk-speak. "Jägerbombs? West, we need to get a couple of Advil down you. I'll call Tim and tell him you're incapacitated."

He pulled her down on top of him. He 'oomphed' when she landed. "My girrrl."

"Your girl."

Then a bubbly cough, and he started snoring. Stacy had never seen West even tipsy. Taking off his shoes and trousers, she then turned him on his side and pancaked him in the bedspread. He would freak in the morning, germ-freak that he was, knowing he slept on top of the bedspread.

Deciding to sleep on the pullout to keep an eye on him, she got ready for bed and called Tim to inform him of West's condition.

"He never gets drunk, Stace. Damn! I miss everything. Could you get me a video?"

"I think you value your ass, Tim. So do I. I'll pretend I didn't hear that. It's this town. I can't wait to get back to Palm Springs. I miss you."

They expressed their love, bantered a bit more, and hung up.

Before bed, she assembled the hangover kit by West's bed. Two bottles of water, more Advil and a piece of fruit.

Before she drifted off to sleep, the question occurred to her whether West had charmed her name out of Mary's mouth, or whether Mary got West snozzled first. Stace betted on the latter.

Chapter Seven

"She's angling for cash. You know that, right?"

West and Stacy sipped tea. His, peppermint for the belly and head. Hers, full-throttle caffeine. They had just come back to the room after breakfast. Stacy had tried to return the favor and bring breakfast up. West refused. Although he was hurting, he didn't want to admit it.

He'd guzzled the water, downed the Advil, and then lurched out of bed and stumbled to the bathroom. The drugs came back up too, so Stacy got some more. She hoped these would stay down.

The second set did. West didn't attempt to talk, so she didn't ask any questions. Any change in air pressure probably caused him pain at that moment.

They sipped tea in the room. West had related how her former mother, now aunt, had drunk him under the table and given nothing away. It was then Stacy supplied the opinion that Mary was after money.

Sarge knocked, and Stacy let him in. He was carrying a smelly concoction and had a slightly evil sparkle in his dishwater-blue eyes. "Drink this."

Stacy recognized the smell. It was a hangover cure he'd made for others who were hurting.

West eyed him and the drink suspiciously, sniffed and recoiled. "Not happening."

Sarge chuffed, did the male thing. "Pansy."

West smiled, then winced. Then attempted to smile again, with less strength behind it. "Yes, I am. Tim wouldn't like it if I changed teams."

Sarge made that almost-laugh sound again. "It's a prairie oyster. Egg, tomato juice, Worcestershire and Tabasco sauce. It'll burn the mornin' after right out of ya. Come on, down it, Westcott."

West eyed it again. He must have been really hurting as Stacy could see him considering it. He took a breath and downed it. For a moment, his whole body shuddered and both Sarge and Stace moved so they weren't blocking West's path to the toilet.

The moment passed. West blinked a few times. Breathed. After a few minutes while Stacy and Sarge talked about inconsequential things, he nodded to Sarge. "That is better."

"I was just saying to West that I think Mary's after money."

Sarge shook his head. "I don' think so, Stace. I think she's downright scared. Those Patriot people are not playing with a full deck, an' they've got guns. She stole a kid. Plus she left. Those people don't take kindly to that kinda stuff."

Stacy explained how she was now conflicted about Mary; she was thankful Mary had taken her away from that place, which slightly mellowed her resentment about the neglectful and unloving upbringing. Stacy felt that once she could get past the emotion, logic would prevail.

"She got messed up in those... whatchamacallits?" Sarge paused, then found the word he was searching for. "Formative years. She passed it down a generation. She may be your aunt by blood, but she is your mom. Mothered you in a piss-poor way, but she's yer mom."

"We'll offer her money." West finally spoke and looked like he was faring better. Water bottle number six or seven was in his hand. "We'll see if we can buy the scared out of her."

Sarge nodded. "If not, I have a Plan B. Don' want to use it so I won't tell you about it."

Mary was off on Saturdays and Sundays. They took Sarge's vehicle. Stacy couldn't have a driver's license and West was most likely not yet legal to drive.

"She'll be in as rough shape as I am."

"If she's true to form, she'll have had her first Caesar of the day. She avoids hangovers by being a functional alcoholic. Staying drunk."

West got a troubled look on his face. Stacy, concerned, asked, "What?"

He shook his head. "I don't know why, but meeting her makes everything... more visceral. And I don't like her, but... I'm almost jealous of her."

"That's some fucked-up shit, West," Sarge interjected.

Stacy gave West a WTF look. He gave a low chuckle. "I know. Although there isn't any real connection between the two of you, I'm jealous she had so much time with you." His face grew very serious. "You are our daughter."

Stacy's throat got thick with emotion. She reached forward and took his hand.

They arrived at Mary's house. It was a different house than the one Stace grew up in, for which she was thankful. Her brain was close to overdosing on Memory Lane.

It was a tiny little house in the older part of town, similar to the house they grew up in. It had a little glassed-in porch.

Mary lived in quiet chaos. Never dirty, in varying degrees of messy. West was going to need his anti-bacterial gel after this. He didn't have the ability to differentiate between messy and dirty. He was a male Monica from "Friends" when it came to tidiness.

Sarge approached the house and knocked. Hard. It took a few minutes, but Mary wordlessly let them in, squinting in the mid-morning summer sun.

She sat down in the living room. Sarge and Mary followed. West, germaphobe extraordinaire, stayed standing.

She lit up a cigarette. "Before you start, I cain't tell you."

West and Sarge had decided Sarge had a better chance of getting through. He rumbled, "Would money loosen your tongue?"

Non-mom Mary's eyes darted again. Left then right. "I dunno, how much?" She sipped on her hair of the dog.

Sarge looked to West. He nodded. Sarge offered, "Five thousand."

Mary broke into a laugh which turned into a cough. "Five grand? I'm talkin' life-changing money. Hundred thousand, nothin' less."

Stacy started to stand. Sarge put a quelling hand out to stop her. It got her hackles up. Too many dominants spoiled the broth. She smiled to herself; that was almost a cliché. West was rubbing off on her.

Sarge said, "Okay, Mare. Hardball time." He put his hand in his jacket. Pulled out some papers. Stood up and crossed over to hand them to her.

"What's this?"

Sarge sat back down. "It's every loan I've ever given you, Mary. That you've not paid back. I made you sign a simple loan agreement every time. The secon' to last piece of paper is yer notice of termination. The last paper is your eviction notice, as yer more than three months behind on the rent."

Mary's hands shook, most likely not from the DT's. "But…" Then she fell silent. Stacy did feel sorry for her in that moment. Auntie dearest, yes, but in that moment she truly was a victim of her addiction.

Stace wasn't aware Mary had borrowed from Sarge. Mostly because she never thought Sarge was much of a soft touch. He knew full well he'd never get the money back. Pissing money away was Auntie Mom's specialty.

Sarge was putting up a good front. But he did have an affection for Mary. He took care of the broken people around him. Until now, she never thought giving money was part of it. Letting them earn it, yes. Sarge always had said functioning alcoholics made the best bar staff. They might steal a little, drink a little, maybe be late for a shift a time or two. But they always came back to work. They needed to be near the source.

Stacy thought it was more. Something about Sarge himself drew him to the Saloon. He didn't drink himself. Maybe he was a reformed alcoholic. Yet he never tried to stop people from drinking. Her non-mom and the everyday drunks included.

Mary kept looking at the papers. Then she gave Stacy a look of contempt, as if it were her fault. Which, in all fairness, it was. Sort of.

"I've gotten away with it. I don't want to do anythin' to come up on their radar."

"We just need to know your birth name, and Stacy's. I don't give two shits whose social security number you're usin'."

Mary shook her head while her body trembled.

"Mare, do you really think they're looking for you after all these years?"

"They're evil crazy. Who knows what crazy will do?"

West said, "I don't think they will even find out. We just need a starting point for the lawyer, so we have some legal footing."

Mary was backed into a corner that she had no way out of. She looked at Stacy. "My sister's name was Marianne Jonas. You were Anastacia Jonas. Or Roberts if the sack of cow dung counts. I was Shayla." It was obvious it had been years since she said the name. It sounded scratchy as she said it.

West asked, "The father's first name?"

Mary shook her head, and looked defiantly at Sarge. "Go ahead and do all these things. I'm not tellin' his name, never."

Sarge put his hands up in a placating gesture. Then he put his hand out for the papers he handed to Mary. She stood, slightly wobbly, neared Sarge cautiously as if he were a pussy cat who had morphed into a cobra, stretched to hand back the papers and scurried back, downing her Caesar in gulps.

Stacy couldn't help but asking, "I know you didn't want me, didn't want to take care of me, but there's one thing I don't understand—why do you hate me so much?"

Mary didn't look at her, just turned her face to the side, unanswering. The clock ticked loudly in the silence of the house. The rays of sun glinted over the drifting cloud of cigarette smoke. When Mary realized that her silence wouldn't suffice, she finally answered. She shrugged and said as though the answer was obvious, "You kilt my sister."

She then stood to refill her drink and stayed in the kitchen. The message was clear. She couldn't say it; at this point she was probably afraid of antagonizing her landlord. But she wanted them gone.

The post-mortem at Ma's Kitchen didn't bring up anything new. They had the information they wanted. West, unused to being hungover and still a bit shaky, took Sarge's advice and loaded up on greasy food, which Stacy teased him for. She texted Tim asking him to get in touch with their travel agent to arrange flights.

There were a few furtive looks thrown her way but no one came up to talk to her. In typical small-town fashion, the choice was to whisper behind her back. Sarge assessed West's sobriety and let them go, promising to come down soon.

There weren't any direct flights from Missoula, so they chose to fly through Salt Lake City. But going home to Tim was a salve both West and Stacy craved.

Saying goodbye to Bandit Creek the second time was even easier.

Chapter Eight

"It's always amazing what you can do when you have a congressman in your pocket."

Tim said, "I would say you had him by the balls. Because at one time, you did have him by his balls and he really enjoyed it."

West snorked involuntarily. Only Tim could make him laugh unselfconsciously and without vanity. West tangled his fingers in Tim's thick silver chain, which had a pendant: a compass which only showed the direction West, the needle pointed to it. It was Tim's public collar, a sign of commitment and ownership. The silver meant permanence. The collar they used for play was also silver, but locked in the back and said 'Property of West'.

Tim raised his mimosa. "To Stacy Knowles."

She blushed. Tim had taken West's name when they married. Now Stacy had their name too. They had offered to adopt her. Her birth certificate and social security number had the name Anastacia Knowles. She still went by Stacy.

It had only taken four months to process with the help of said congressman. West was a man with many connections, and it helped to grease the wheels.

Mary, unfortunately, had had to have a chat with the FBI and ATF. Even though her information was twenty-four years out of date, they had eagerly interrogated her.

Sometimes it was hard not to feel sorry for Mary. Sometimes it was even harder not to hate her. Stacy had considered going back to the counselor, but felt she learnt enough tools to cope the first time around.

And Brendan. Well, it was a work in progress. He had texted, emailed and voicemailed as promised. Had adhered to every rule and protocol. Surrendered his orgasms to her. She was very stingy with the orgasms at first, but less so now.

Once he was feeling more secure in the relationship the alpha male in him had come back with a vengeance. After Bren had run into Barton Ellis, he questioned her and found out the circumstances of how Stacy came to witness his initiation. Bren had always thought that Stace found out from the high-school mean girls.

Stacy had agreed with Brendan that doing anything to Barton Ellis would come back to his mother and maybe even Mary and Sarge. Not that Sarge gave a rat's ass about the Ellises.

But Brendan swore that Bart would get his comeuppance for his cruelty. Stacy preferred to believe in karma. Potato, potahto. Except she suspected Bren might engineer the karma. If he could get away with it, who was she to argue? This was one situation in which she refused to take the high ground.

Every day her connection to Brendan was growing stronger. She came to accept the fact that they were both products of their childhoods in Bandit Creek. He with an overbearing mother with high expectations, and her growing up with the opposite.

This weekend was the first time she'd allowed him to come visit. His flight was arriving in a few hours. Excitement jangled in her stomach. Arousal too. She craved Brendan.

He was trying to get work in California. Barring that, he wanted to set up roots here and get a place. Oilfield work kept him away from home for long periods of time. Consequently, he had longer break periods and reasoned he could easily set up home here.

Privately, Stacy was pleased but didn't want to get her hopes up for their future. They might not even be sexually compatible in person.

Goddess knew they were very compatible on the phone. The rush she got controlling Bren on the phone sent her into an adrenaline high which happened during a good scene. Stacy could count on one cat-o'-nine-tails the amount of times that had happened sceneing at the club. With Brendan, it happened a often.

West brought her back into the present. "Planning your scene tonight? Are you taking him to the club or at your flat?"

"I think, for tonight, the club."

"Still cautious, Stace?" Tim asked.

"Your birthday present is languishing at your place. It needs to be used or it won't feel loved," West mock-reproached. West and Tim had transformed her spare room into a dungeon. St Andrew's cross, spanking bench, the works.

"It's only going to be used with someone who I'm committed to. You know that."

West sighed melodramatically. "It is such a pain in the ass to raise a Domme. Take a chance, lovey. You know he's earned it."

Stacy had volunteered information from time to time. The couple had revealed to her that a major schism had happened between them at the beginning of their relationship and they had gotten through it. Looking at their domestic bliss, it gave her hope for the future.

"He's never been to a club. Montana has very limited BDSM activity. So it's gatherings at someone's house."

"Sarge said Idaho has lots of perverts like us, though," Tim added.

Stacy leaned against Tim's huge chest, loving the way he made her feel petite. Brendan had filled out a bit, but although he was taller, she would never feel tiny around him. Of course people Tim's size were rare.

He leaned down. "Bring him for Sunday lunch, okay, Stace?"

She turned around for an all-encompassing hug, looked up and nodded. Sundays were family time. Tim and West would give

Brendan the third degree. Ultimately they would leave the decision up to her.

Tim continued. "If you want his first experience to be positive, think again about taking him to your house. I think it would be better for both of you. Less daunting. He's not trained yet. I hope you're going to make his first time more casual."

Stacy kept turning Tim's words in her mind for the rest of the day. By the time she was driving to the airport, she'd acquiesced.

This was about making Brendan's first Dominance/submission experience a positive one. It wasn't about her needs.

She'd forgotten it, until Tim had reminded her. Up until now, it had been all about delayed orgasm games, which she loved. Perhaps they should practice in person what they had been doing on the phone first.

They'd discussed hard and soft limits. Things Brendan wouldn't do–extreme pain, humiliation, etc. And soft limits–anal. She didn't like scening with pain sluts and humiliation whores herself. As for anal, well, it was something she truly enjoyed. The orgasm a male sub got from anal was intense. Hopefully there would be time in the future for that.

Once decided, she was excited about breaking in her dungeon. Letting him into her sanctuary, her home, was a huge deal. Stacy was the type of person who didn't answer the door unless the person called first.

Her sanctum. Her domain. Her territory. It was because she hadn't ever had a place that was solely hers. Tim and West never entered her room without permission.

Brendan was staying at Agua Caliente Casino, a nearby hotel. Just because she'd decided to give him dungeon rights didn't mean he was staying over.

She watched Bren walk out in the airport, wearing button-fly jeans, another soft t-shirt. This one was plum and it seemed to make his eyes even greener.

He had a way of sauntering. Not rushed, but not meandering either. Taking everything in. He always had the talent of looking like he wanted to be wherever he was.

He fit here. She could see him living in Palm Springs. Stacy tried to put the thought aside. Looking at him, how his smile lit up when he spotted her—she knew she was fucked if it didn't work out.

In that moment, Stace accepted the fact she'd fallen for him again. If this weekend went well, she would allow Brendan to discuss a future together. Something she had put the kibosh on when he consistently brought it up.

He came up and stood there. Then he shrugged, dropped his carry-on bag to the floor and hugged her. He smelled like his toothpaste and clean sweat. Minty and musky. Undertones of soap underneath.

Stacy relaxed into the hug. It felt so good, being in the shelter of his strong arms. Being a Domme didn't mean being a hardass all the time. Something else had gotten hard when they were hugging though, which pleased her. She loved having an immediate effect on him. Physical reaction trumped sincere words every time when it came to attraction. Telling someone you're attracted to them is one thing. A straining hard-on is proof. She was tempted to have a feel to see if Brendan had followed her "go commando" order.

The hug lasted a long time.

Stacy put her hand out after the embrace and he picked up his bag and clasped her hand.

She dropped him off to settle in at the hotel, to pick him up later. She had some work to do at home.

***

Brendan felt jittery. He was usually unflappable. His dick had been hard from the moment he had seen Stacy. Seeing her in the September desert sun, even more comfortable in her skin than last time, made him rise to attention.

Cee had stunning eyes, full lips, honeyed voice. Plus an hourglass figure a pin-up would envy. But ever since they had reached puberty, she'd had an innate sexiness which had little to do with her features.

It wasn't intentional on her part, but her sexiness made him hard. Had been the cause of a million jack-offs. Sometimes, he even had flings with look-a-likes. Until he realized the similarity ended there.

Tonight. Tonight. Scared. Excited. Both emotions messing with his nerves. Making smooth motor control near impossible.

He couldn't fathom to this day why he craved sexual submission. He was a confident man, wasn't cowed by anyone. The oilfield had a lot of blowhard bosses. He stood up to them easily.

But in the bedroom, to give up personal power was amazing. He had finally figured out a major part of it. Watching a strong woman control his physical being was a sexual high. Pleasing Cee was the ultimate goal, and the ultimate rush.

He waited outside the Casino in the warm dusk, wearing casual clothes as ordered, waiting for Cee to pick him up. He didn't have to wait long. She was wearing a blue semi-transparent top and a flowy skirt. Not too dressy.

The trip was short, to a small two-story apartment complex. So not the club then. He let out a breath he hadn't known he was holding.

She took his hand again. That little intimacy meant so much.

On the ground level at the end of the hall, she unlocked the door and let him in. It was roomy, airy, without clutter and filled with artwork. Cee always did love art.

She gave him a quick tour, and then led him to a room. Inside it was a mini-dungeon. He'd done a lot of research and learned quite a bit when he tested the waters before. There was a massage table, a small St. Andrew's Cross and a spanking bench. Strangely, a loveseat in one corner.

"This is just going to be a training session. Your first." She smiled, almost shyly but not quite. "Hopefully there are going to be many more. You won't truly submit to me. It takes time. We're just exploring here, okay?"

His nerves spiked. He started to breathe faster. She led him to the massage table, her warm soft hands pushing him. On closer inspection, it was more like a table he had seen in a doctor's office. His hair was standing on end and he felt cold. "Give me your shirt. Lie face up for me, Bren, okay?"

He nodded spastically. His nipples pebbled in the warm air.

"What color are you at, Bren?"

She'd told him to gauge his feelings by the traffic light system. Red was the safeword. The scene would stop and there would be no more sexual play that day if the safeword was said. It motivated a person to be really sure before they said it. Yellow was discomfort. They would discuss the discomfort. Green was all good.

"Green. Scared shitless, but green."

Her eyes flashed with something that made his insides all warm and safe. "Green what, Bren?"

"Miss."

"Good. Now, for now, we're going to discard green. Make an okay sign with your hand. Good. I'll make that sign when I'm checking on you. If you're green, you'll do it back. If not, say yellow or red. If at any time you are at yellow or red, tell me. Communication is very important." Her smooth, quiet voice commanded him. Intimately she leaned against his shoulder. "There's no reason to be scared, Bren. I would never hurt you."

"It's not quite that sort of scared, Miss." As he lay on the table, his dick got harder, anticipating. The base of his spine tingled.

"Talk to me. Dominance and submission is all about communication. What kind of scared?"

He tried to think it through in his head, but he wasn't really firing on all cylinders right now. "I want this. I so want this. But it's sort of like losing your virginity, you know?"

Cee kissed his forehead, and he calmed at the touch. "I am so grateful, Brendan, that you chose to save your submission for me."

She retrieved two rubber circles out of her pocket. "Now stay still, Bren."

Cee traced her fingertips around his nipples, gently pinching one, and then the other. He couldn't stifle a groan. It was taking all his strength not to force his hips upward.

Tracing down to his button fly, with excruciating slowness, she unbuttoned him.

Stacy loved Brendan's reaction. His groans went straight to her nether regions, and she felt her inner muscles clench. His voice was amazing. His groans, oh, his groans zinged under her belly, giving her butterflies and pre-orgasmic tension. It wouldn't take much to get her off after she took care of him.

She took hold of his hard cock, hot to the touch. Lubricated at the end. Wet with pre-come. The tremors in his body increased. She made the 'okay' sign, which he mirrored. "Remember, Bren, if you're close to coming, tell me. You aren't allowed to come without permission. This thick, hard cock is mine."

He rasped, "Yes, Miss."

Miss sounded so fucking fantastic from those light pink lips. After she applied the cock ring, she kept her hand there as she leaned up and took a kiss from him.

Stacy kissed him gently, close-mouthed to begin, enjoying the wet soft warmth of his lips. He opened up and questingly pushed his tongue forward. She opened, deepening the kiss. Gentle deepness. Affectionate. Swallowing his groan when she started squeezing the base of his cock above the ring.

"Miss..." he whispered into her mouth. Stacy ended the kiss. Looked in his eyes. "I'm already getting close."

She took her hand off. Went back down to his cock. Checked they were still 'green'. She motioned him to lift his hips, taking his jeans off.

His legs were hairy and very muscular. His hipbones jutted out. Stacy traced his legs from hip to feet. Remembering his ticklishness, she didn't touch the bottoms of his feet.

While she belted his ankles to the table his breathing increased, but he motioned her to go on. She then put cuffs on his wrists. Moving his arms above his head, she pulled his arms taut, chaining them to o-rings in the wall. She completed his restraint by belting his hips to the table. "Now you won't have to restrain yourself."

Brendan was feeling jittery and logically he knew it was because he couldn't fucking move. But he trusted Cee, and couldn't imagine why he was shivering. He could feel the burn where his muscles stretched over his ribs.

He could feel every piece of leather holding him down, knowing that in Cee's mind, every restraint was an embrace from her.

He lifted his head up to look down his body, dick standing to attention in the middle. Cee adjusted the table and started spreading his legs. It made him feel so open, vulnerable.

Brendan felt the pressure increase when Cee put another ring around the base of his ball sac. But even though he felt closer to coming, he felt more in control.

Every nerve was alive. The smells and sounds of the small dungeon were vivid. He smelled a burnt herb of some sort and heard soft classical music playing. The creaking of the leather restraints intensified his feelings. Brendan felt light-headed, but not unpleasantly so.

Then Cee lightly scratched between his legs. She massaged a point behind his testicles. "Oh god, Miss, oh fuck!" He tried to fuck the air, his dick twitching. His balls tightened, preparing to shoot. "I'm close again, Miss!"

She squeezed the middle of his concrete-hard dick with a slightly painful pressure. The need to come wasn't as urgent. "Watch me."

She took her top off. Her beautiful full breasts were encased in a balcony bra and the nipples were half visible and looked hard. When she removed her skirt, he noticed the thong panties matched her bra. Also blue like her eyes. Her belly button was pierced and had a long pendant resting on her soft belly. He could smell the musk of her excitement. He was doing that to her. His dick pulsed with his heart. The pressure was increasing.

She took her bra off. Cee's nipples were tightly bumped. The panties came last. Not a hair to be seen. A lot of women did it today, to increase sensation.

She was sexy. Confident. Beautiful. She walked to him, bent over, her nipple brushing his mouth. He sucked it softly, increasing the pressure slowly, reveling in her taste. She tasted sweet and tart at the same time. Moaning, she pulled away, changed nipples, her soft groans increasing in volume, her musky scent getting stronger.

He wanted to touch her with his body, his hands holding her breasts. Craved the heavy weight of them so much his palms itched. He accepted, mostly, it wasn't his to decide. Hoped she would let him come. Preferably inside her.

Cee pulled away, face flushed, pupils dilated. There was a sexy, calculating smile on her face. She was glowing. He had a feeling of contentment knowing that he was the cause of that smile.

Stacy almost came when she had Bren suckling her nipples. She'd always thought it was possible as they were sensitive.

Three more times she had brought him to the brink of orgasm. Pre-come weeping, adding to the lubrication.

The delayed orgasm torture was taking its toll. She didn't want to restrict his blood flow much longer. She unfastened his hands, climbed on the table and straddled his body in a reverse cowgirl position, hovering over his torso instead of his cock. "Put your hand there." Twisting back, she gestured underneath her pussy. Brendan moved his right hand underneath. Stacy then instructed him to place the heel of his hand on her clit. "Don't move."

It wasn't going to take her much. The coiling in her lower belly signaled how close she was.

"So wet, you're so hot and wet," Bren murmured over and over.

Stacy lubed up her hands and interlocked her fingers around his cock. Her vaginal walls clenched. Anticipating bringing him over the brink. Watching his hips work against their restraint. She started slowly, quickly building up momentum.

Brendan's groans increased; another shot of pre-come came out. Stacy could feel his hot breath whispering against her buttocks. She let go of her own control and started grinding against his palm. He pushed, trying to increase her pleasure. Against instruction, but something she would think about later. It was all about their pleasure right now.

"Oh fuck, oh fuck, fuck, fuck, I can't, I can't hold..."

"Let go, Brendan, you have permission to let go."

Come streamed out of his penis, jerking and spasming, once, twice, again, again. Each spurt hit her belly, whilst his hips rotated out as far open as the restraints allowed. She concentrated on her contractions, squeezing, breathing, jutting into Brendan's hand. The muscles in her belly squeezed from all sides at the same time, her pelvis tilting forward and up in the direction of her belly button. She came in long juddering cycles, the insides of her legs spasming, her toes pointed, soaking his belly and hand.

She let out a throaty laugh, lying back. She knew that Brendan would cradle her. They lay there for a moment, his strong arms encircling her. She could feel his chest rising and falling rapidly, as if he'd run a race. Neither seemed capable of speech.

The moment passed and she shakily got off the table, removed his cock ring from the still semi-hard penis. She made eye contact. "You okay?"

He rasped, "Green, Miss, so very green."

She laughed again, moving to his ankle restraints, massaging where he pulled against them. They hadn't been tight enough to restrict blood flow. Finally, she released his perfect torso. She pulled him to a seated position, slowly. Stacy led him to the loveseat. Got him to lie down.

Brendan felt like he had just run a marathon whilst experiencing the best orgasm of his life. Cee was rubbing his body with lotion, bringing him down after their scene.

Then she spooned him. The press of her breasts in his back stirred his dick, which by all rights should be dead. The dick might be willing, but the intimacy of this moment was a different kind of high.

Finally she said, in her soft silky voice, "How do you feel?"

He turned around and brought her deep into his arms, her lips pressing against his chest, her musk mixing with Brendan's.

"Happy. Hopeful. I love you, Stace."

Their relationship was growing roots again. Getting stronger. She felt ready to trust him. She had accepted he had been an incredibly stupid teenager trying to live in the huge shadow of his father. Danica Thomas really did a number on Brendan. Stacy still had scar tissue around her heart, but her mind was open to the possibilities. Her heart would take a bit longer.

He felt her lips move, hopefully into a smile. "Cee," she said. "Call me Cee."

Thank You!

I hope you enjoyed "Twice Shy". Stay tuned for the next book, Twice Bitten (Restraint Series #2), for a continuation of Stacy and Bren. The book also gives us a look into Sarge's shady past.

Read a bit further, I've included a snippet of Bren's training scene from the next book, available in August 2014.

Do you want to be notified of upcoming releases? You can sign up for the Swords & Lips Newsletter at http://www.jillcflanagan.com/swordsandlips

Catch up with Stacy and her chosen family!
Read an excerpt from
Twice Bitten
Out in August 2014!

If there was one thing that Stacy despised, it was not having control. The other thing she hated was having someone touch what was hers. And Brendan was hers. She knew that Tomas wouldn't make a pass. She also knew that the arousal that came from Brendan wasn't directed at Tomas.

Tomas agreed to train Brendan. And she was observing. Which was the first mistake. She couldn't help herself. West had told her politely that it would be torture to see it. Because Tomas was a very talented Dominant. Extremely talented.

As much as she wanted to be the one training Brendan, it wasn't wise. Her heart was soft to him. She wouldn't be strong enough in the beginning to go test his limits.

One look into those eyes, one raspy breath from that sexy, smoke-damaged voice and she would capitulate.

Brendan thought he knew what it was to submit. He didn't realize that he'd not even come close to submitting yet.

She couldn't stay. But leaving was going to be hell. She supposed it would be like leaving your child at daycare for the first time. She snorted silently when a visual image of 'Dommy Daycare' flashed in her brain, a gaggle of subs corralled by leather and PVC clad Doms and Dommes.

They'd discussed his training. Communication was key in any relationship, but it was essential in D/s one. He said that he understood that she couldn't stay. But he was nervous. Being dominated by a man, even an arrow-straight man like Tomas weirded him out.

This was a test. For both of them. Sighing, she slowly stood, walked toward the man she loved. The man had snuck back into her heart. Scared shitless. Sure Bren was, too.

She walked quietly, in a flowing dress that stopped just above the knees. Her knee high suede boots with small heels showed off her shapely legs. Just as her dress showcased and showed a considerable amount of her full breasts.

Brendan was restrained, tied to a St. Andrew's cross. Blindfolded him. Inducting him with silence, and had ordered silence unless he was to utter his safe word.

As she walked forward, Tomas gave her an appreciative up and down. She liked dressing like a woman, not a catwoman. She liked the way her curves pleasantly flowed in retro dresses and waist cinchers.

Tomas had tried to talk her into trying the submissive side permanently with him at one time. He knew it was a lost cause when he tried, but it had been pleasant being chased for that month.

Tomas had trained her too. According to Tim and West's rules, all players in the club have to be trained. And Dominants also have to have a day of experiencing submissiveness. Also known as 'sucky submissive day' in her mind.

She looked him in the eyes and gave him a knowing smile. She tilted her head, in askance. He nodded.

She approached Bren. Placed a palm on his back. He tensed, and then relaxed as he recognized either her touch or her scent. Maybe her presence. She whispered in his ear, slightly biting it first. Loving his physical and emotional reaction to her. "Bren, I'm leaving now." His breathing increased, distressed. "You'll be fine. I promise." She paused, looking at his skin, looking at the dampness. The sick-sweat appearing from fear. "Do you trust me?" He took a couple of shallow breaths, and then a deeper one. "Then trust me to give you the best trainer. Tomas is. He will not touch you in a sexual way. But are allowed to come when he orders it though. You are not allowed to feel ashamed for getting turned on." Stacy bit the ear again, harder, licked to soothe the bite. Sighed into his ear, "I don't want to boost your ego or anything, but let me tell you something. I love you. I'm not sure that I want to yet. But I do. We have a long way to go. Dominance and submission are important to me and I need to know how far we can go with that." She then kissed his neck gently. "I'll come get you in 90 minutes."

Turning around and schooling her face into a flat expression, she regretfully walked out of the room. Sucky timing, she thought. Finally admitting to him that she loved him and leaving him to be dominated by someone else.

Want to read more of Jill C Flanagan's work?
The **Gilt Series (Prequel & Book 1)** out April 2014
Gilt•y –will be **free** for a limited time!
Sign up for the Swords & Lips Newsletter to find out when it's free!

Gilt•y – Prequel out April 2014

Ash needs to make money. Her brother is going to trial, her sister is pregnant, her mother's health isn't great and her father is a dreamer who spends all their savings on the next best thing.

Good thing she was brought up to con people. Even better that she has always had a little bit of 'mind magic' as her Mam calls it.

Small cons are all she's ever done. This time her family needs a big chunk of cash and the best way to do that is a long con.

The target? A honeypot scheme involving a powerful man running for Senator. .

And the Senatorial candidate's Communications Officer? Too bad he's the first guy she's been interested in, well, forever.

Even though politics are dangerous, politicians may be deadly.

Gilt•ed - out April 2014

It's been over five years since she's been in the same room Keithley "Lee' Hierne, black hat hacker turned white collar cyber-strategist. She's made a new life for her sister and herself.

Lee makes a reappearance in her life, threatening the stable quiet life she's managed to assemble.

Putting her livelihood at risk is his first move.

She's already proved that she will do anything for family. And it's a character flaw he will exploit to get what he wants – for Ash to use her 'mind magic' for his agenda.

If only the risks were only her pride. Unfortunately the choice is between her family and her soul...